To:——————————

From:——————————

On:——————————

——————————

——————————

To: The People's Trust for Endangered Species
Hares are becoming increasingly scarce in Britain.
If you would like to help, write to:

PTES
15 Cloisters House
8 Battersea Park Road
London SW8 4BG

CW

MYRIAD BOOKS LIMITED
35 Bishopsthorpe Road, London SE26 4PA

First published in 2002 by
PICCADILLY PRESS LIMITED
5 Castle Road, London NW1 8PR
www.piccadillypress.co.uk

Text copyright © Adèle Geras 2002
Illustrations copyright © Cliff Wright 2002

ISBN 1 905606 16 8
EAN 9 781905 606 160

Designed by Mark Mills

Printed in China

Wishes For You

Adèle Geras

illustrated by
Cliff Wright

MYRIAD BOOKS LIMITED

I wish you . . .

Light from behind the hill
spilling into the sky.

Kisses to wake you,

warm sun on your face.

A path that goes from here
to everywhere.
Daydreams like birds
unfolding wide white wings.

A kind gaze following you
as you walk.

A smile to smile at when you
turn your head.

Trees wide enough
for you to
hide behind
and drifting
shadows, pieces
of the dark . . .

. . . which vanish
as the sun
moves through
the leaves.

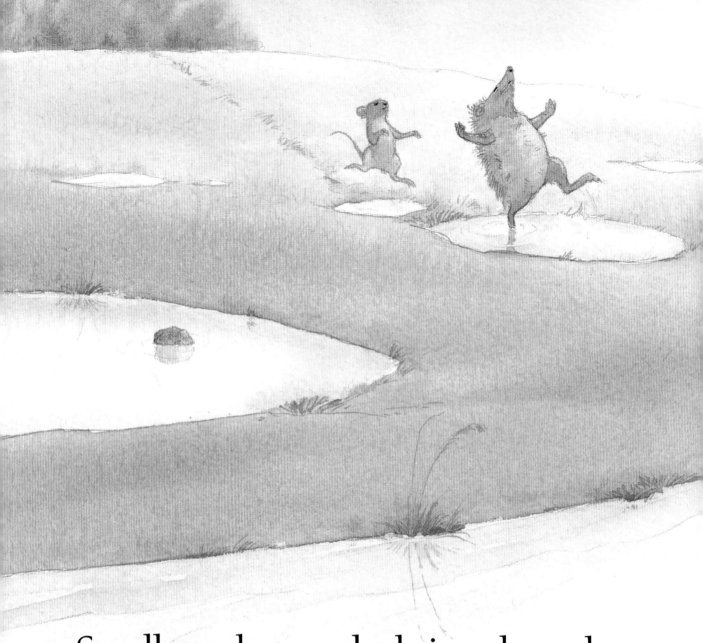

Small pools to splash in when the
rain comes down.
A dancing stream to follow with
your dance.

Your own hands strong to pile up stones you find into a tower high enough to climb . . .

... and arms outstretched

to catch you if you fall.

Someone to tell you words
for everything.
Laughter to join your laughter,
songs to sing.

A quilt to cover you
and all your dreams,

warm in your bed,

safe through the quiet night.

Darkness and moonlight,

your star in the sky.